LOST IN DARKNESS

DUEL MASTERS™

LOST IN DARKNESS

SCHOLASTIC INC.

NEW YORK   TORONTO   LONDON   AUCKLAND   SYDNEY
MEXICO CITY   NEW DELHI   HONG KONG   BUENOS AIRES

ISBN 0-439-66320-2

Published by Scholastic Inc.
SCHOLASTIC and associated logos are trademarks and/or registered trademarks of Scholastic Inc.

12 11 10 9 8 7 6 5 4 3 2 1   4 5 6 7 8 9/0

Printed in the U.S.A.
First printing, September 2004

INTRODUCTION

The world as we know it isn't the world around us. There are awesome creatures living in five mysterious civilizations, realms of Nature, Fire, Water, Light, and Darkness. They can be brought into our world through an incredible card game — Duel Masters!

Though many kids and adults play this game, only the best can call forth these creatures. They are known as *Kaijudo Masters*.

This is the story of one junior duelist, or *Senpai*, unique among all others. His name is Shobu Kirifuda.

A thin shaft of light slashed across the Master's dark office. As he peered through the slim opening in the curtains, his mind was not on what he saw outside.

"I know you're anxious to see the boy's true talent," urged Knight from behind the Master, "but I don't think this is a good idea." There was unusual stress in his normally icy-cool tone.

"Why not?" asked the Master.

"He's not ready to duel with a member of the Temple," Knight replied.

The Master turned. As always, the hood of his robe and his long hair hid most of his face. He answered Knight firmly. "That is for me to decide."

"But it is my job to advise you," Knight shot back, "and I think we should go slowly with this one. Sure, he defeated Jamira last week, but Shobu is just realizing his talent. We don't want to turn him off before we know the full extent of his power."

"That's the point," said the Master. "It's important to learn what he's capable of."

"I agree," Knight said, "but for the boy's sake as well as ours, let's not rush —"

"I don't think you're hearing me," the Master interrupted firmly. "Our goal is to discover Kaijudo Masters, using whatever means necessary."

"But Shobu is special," countered Knight, squinting through his sunglasses. They were hardly necessary in the dark office.

"You will do as you are told!" ordered the

Master. "Shori Kirafuda's son is valuable. I intend to have him, and you will not get in my way! Do we understand each other?"

"Yes, we do, sir," said Knight with a sigh, "but let's hope Shobu's inexperience doesn't leave him in the dark."

The Master's strong jaw jutted out firmly. "You're his mentor, Knight. Be certain he doesn't become lost in darkness!"

In the card shop across town, Shobu Kirafuda's mood was anything but dark. He was hanging out with his pals Sayuki, Mimi, Rekuta, and Rekuta's dad, who owned the store. Well, "hanging out" wasn't exactly the right term. Shobu was flying across the room, doing cartwheels over the new pack of Duel Masters cards he'd just opened.

"This is fantastic!" Shobu shouted. "I got Reusol, the Oracle. And Aqua Hulcus. Onslaughter Triceps and Poisonous Mushroom, too! And best of all . . . Gatling Skyterror!"

New to Duel Masters, Mimi asked innocently, "Gatling Skyterror? Is that a good card?"

Sayuki rolled her eyes. "Can't you tell from Shobu's reaction? I mean, seriously. We go through this every time he gets a new pack of cards! It's cute and yet disturbing at the same time."

Rekuta nodded. "He definitely lives to own the zone. Borders on obsession."

Rekuta's father smiled. "Ah, but what a beautiful obsession! That boy's going to be a Kaijudo Master some day. Mark my words."

Shobu continued to jump crazily. "Who's the man? Yes! Whoo-hoo! Who will my deck demolish today?"

Rekuta's father took a small piece of folded paper from his pocket. "I might have the answer to that question, Shobu. Perhaps someone's already challenged you."

Shobu stopped short. "Huh? What do you

mean?"

"A terrifying duelist showed up here today," Rekuta's father explained.

"A t-t-terrifying duelist?" Mimi whimpered, with a shudder.

"That's what I said," declared the shop owner, nodding. "He was a sharp dresser — wore a stylish suit. The kids dueling at the time taunted him. Called him Tie Boy. He just smiled and then destroyed them all . . . one duel at a time. This guy was good. Really good. His deck was full of Nature Civilization and Light Civilization cards. And he knew how to use them!"

Rekuta's father passed the paper to Shobu. "He left this for you."

Shobu took the note. "He's probably a friend of Jamira's, trying to avenge his buddy's humbling loss to me last week."

"That was a terrific duel," marveled Sayuki.

"You can say that again!" agreed Rekuta.

"It's got to be some kind of honor-vendetta thing," said Shobu, opening the note. His eyes bugged as he read the message. "Whoa! Hey, listen to this, guys! 'Dear Shobu. Your Duel Masters deck stinks and your father was a second-rate player. Meet me at the park at four o'clock PM tomorrow for a duel. Your sworn mortal enemy, Toru.'"

Rekuta shook his head and whistled. "That guy plans to take you down, Shobu!"

"I know," said Shobu with a smile. "But I never turn down a challenge."

A gentle breeze blew through the park the next day, occasionally causing Toru's necktie to flap. While his suit was dressy and cool, his mood was heating up with impatience. He was tired of waiting for Shobu. Checking his watch, Toru muttered, "Where is this whiz kid Kirafuda? Can't a challenge ever start on time? Is nothing sacred? Probably trying to psych me out by making me wait."

Toru's thoughts were interrupted by a sinister voice behind him. "Got nothing better to do than talk to yourself, buddy?"

Toru turned to face a spooky sight — a boy

with an evil grin. The stranger wore black leather pants and a long, matching coat with the collar up. His black hair spilled over his shoulders. The coat wasn't buttoned, and it blew open to reveal a bare chest. Though Toru sounded tough in his note to Shobu, compared to this guy, he was a powder puff!

"I see you're packing your Duel Masters deck," said the stranger. "Why don't you duel with me?"

"I can't," Toru said. "I've got a game scheduled."

"What are you afraid of?" taunted the stranger.

"I told you," repeated Toru, "I've got something planned. The little jerk should be here any minute."

The evil grin crossed the stranger's face again. "Don't worry. It will be a short duel. I promise."

"Your taunts won't change my mind," said Toru.

"Would an insult work?" the stranger asked.

"Depends on the insult," Toru shot back.

"How about, *I don't know which is worse . . . your hairstyle or that ugly tie*?"

That pushed Toru to his limit. "You have no idea what you've just gotten yourself into. I'm a member of the Temple."

The stranger sneered. "Ooh, that explains your outfit."

"You're not in any position to knock the suit . . . you loser in leather!" exclaimed Toru.

"Just shuffle your deck, pretty boy," the stranger said with a cackle, "and prepare to meet the darkness."

4

Shobu raced toward the park in a panic. Sayuki, Rekuta, and Mimi struggled to keep up with him.

Rekuta carried the laptop that he used for tracking all of Shobu's moves in duels. Running as fast as his stubby legs could carry him, he panted heavily and called out, "Slow down, Shobu!"

"Can't stop, Rekuta," Shobu shouted over his shoulder. "We're late!"

"We are not late, duel boy," said Sayuki. "You are the one who got detention for playing with your

Duel Masters deck in class!"

"I had to prepare for today's duel with Toru," said Shobu.

"What duel?" asked Mimi. "He probably figured you were scared of him and left long ago."

Hearing that, Shobu ran even faster. "I can't have people thinking I was afraid to face him!"

The group finally arrived at the park, relieved to find an opponent still waiting for Shobu. It was a dark stranger sporting a slimy smile. He was shirtless under a black leather jacket.

Shobu flashed Toru's note. "Hey, Toru, thanks for the written invitation. I'm answering in person!"

The stranger only let out a grim laugh.

"You going to giggle all day or play cards?" taunted Shobu.

"I was just trying to postpone your agony," replied the sinister stranger.

"So show me what you got!" demanded

Shobu.

The two shuffled each other's decks, dealt their cards, and the duel was on!

Shobu was surprised to see Darkness Civilization cards coming out of his opponent's hand. *Whoa!* he thought. *Rekuta's dad said this guy was good with Nature Civilization and Light Civilization cards! Something's not right here.*

"Are you sure that's the deck you want to use?" Shobu asked.

"The last time I checked, nimrod!" the stranger shot back. "Worry about your own lame deck and duel!"

"Well, in that case, I'm super sure I'm going to beat you!" bragged Shobu.

K night always looked smooth in his trademark sunglasses, and whenever he drove his hot, red sports car, he was off-the-charts hip. But as he sped toward the park, he had more on his mind than his coolness. He'd stopped by Rekuta's father's card shop earlier, figuring he'd find Shobu there. He wanted to observe the young duelist's progress at a distance. Rekuta's father had told Knight about Toru's challenge to duel Shobu. Knight had immediately hopped in his car and zoomed toward the park.

What Shobu doesn't know is that Toru is the second most powerful duelist at the Temple, Knight thought. *The Master must have set this whole thing up against my wishes. Shobu may be facing a world of pain. He's not ready to get in the zone with someone of Toru's caliber! I seriously need to re-think this mentor thing!*

Knight was met by a very bizarre sight when he arrived at the park. It was Toru — stumbling along the sidewalk like a zombie. His mouth hung open and his eyes were more glazed over than a couple of stale donuts! The dude was really messed up!

"Toru! What happened?" asked Knight.

"I dueled," mumbled Toru. "Got destroyed."

Knight was shocked. "Shobu beat you?"

"No. A challenger. An evil maniac. Never seen him before."

"What did he look like?" asked Knight.

"Black leather," Toru replied. "Long, straight hair. Laughed like a vampire. It was horrible. Beat me like a drum. Like I was a beginner. Told me there was much more where that came from."

"He was just trying to psych you out, Toru," Knight said soothingly. "Don't let him get into your head."

Toru kept mumbling. "It was like my cards were sucked into the darkness."

Knight laughed nervously. "Don't worry, friend. You'll get over this. No cards were sucked into the darkness! See? Your deck is still in your hand."

Toru tossed his cards aside and walked away. "They're in the bushes now. I may never duel again."

Knight felt blown away by what he'd just seen. "If this guy can destroy Toru, what would he do to Shobu?"

6

"I attack with Fatal Attacker Horvath!" shouted Shobu.

The dark stranger's attitude had changed since the start of the game. He was losing bad. "I lost another shield!" he moaned.

But Rekuta wasn't buying his act. He leaned toward Sayuki and whispered, "This dude is acting. He's pretending to be a bad player to sucker Shobu into a false sense of security."

"Well, if that's true," Sayuki observed, "his little plan might backfire. He's in a big hole unless he has a secret comeback strategy."

Knight ran up behind them. "His comeback strategy is that he isn't Toru!"

Everyone's eyes bugged at that news, except the dark dueler's. His eyes twinkled with maniacal delight.

"So who are you, Mr. Strange Mystery Dueler?" Shobu asked. "I'm guessing by your evil laugh that you're a bad guy."

The stranger sneered and pointed a bony finger at Shobu. "You shouldn't stereotype people that way."

"So you're not a bad guy?" Shobu pressed.

"Of course I am," admitted the stranger.

"I should have known!" cried Rekuta. "You're not even wearing a shirt."

"Like the purple one your little buddy, Show Boy . . . er, Shobu . . . is wearing?"

"Don't change the subject. Your bad-guy

black leather outfit is a dead give-away!" Sayuki exclaimed.

Possessing the most fashion sense, Mimi said, "And your hairstyle just screams evil maniac!"

The stranger cackled. "I prefer 'evil genius,' if you don't mind."

"So you have some wicked plan in place?" asked Shobu.

"Of course I do!" answered the stranger. "But I can't tell you everything up front. What would we have to talk about later?"

"Then where's Toru?" asked Shobu.

"Our little tune-up for his match with you ended in his destruction," the stranger replied. "Poor little fellow could barely walk away. What can I say? My mind games and Darkness deck were too much for him."

Knight finally recognized the stranger. "Darkness deck . . . Wait a minute! I've heard about you. You must be . . ."

"King of the world," interrupted the stranger.

"You're Kyoshiro Kokujo!" exclaimed Knight. "You've gotten a lot of attention in the duel world lately. Negative attention!"

"Well, there's no such thing as bad publicity," said Kokujo smugly.

"I've heard you like to show up at duels and challenge the strongest player in the room," said Knight. "At first you act like you don't know what you're doing. But then something happens. A weirdness creeps into your opponents' minds. Those who duel you feel like they're being sucked into darkness. And then they never want to play again!"

"That can't be true!" exclaimed Rekuta.

Kokujo giggled. "I'm afraid it is. Talk to Toru."

Knight nodded nervously. "A lot of players are leaving the dueling world because of this guy."

"So this is your evil plan, Kokujo?" Shubo

asked.

"Please, call me Ko, little friend!" urged the dark one. "And yes, my plan is simple, yet quite effective. I want to rid the Duel Masters world of cute little imposters like you who claim they're great."

That hit a nerve with Shobu. "Then let's see who can walk their talk, Ko, baby!" he fired back. "I attack with Stonesaur! Break his shields!"

"Good move, Shobu!" cheered Rekuta. "Let's teach this guy a lesson!"

"You've almost won, Shobu," Sayuki urged. "Put him away!"

But Ko just smiled. "I think it's time to get serious, schoolboy. Recess is over."

7

Knight scanned the dueling board. *Winning won't be as easy as Shobu thinks*, he realized. *He's ahead in swift attacks, but Ko has a lot of mana. He's leading Shobu into a trap. As his mentor, I have to let him learn on his own. But will he be swallowed into Ko's darkness?*

Knight snapped out of his thoughts as Ko made his next move. "I summon Gigargon!"

Shobu laughed. "That's a lame move. Gigargon's weak and . . ." Shobu's mouth dropped open. He suddenly understood.

"Your ignorance is only surpassed by your overconfidence, Show Boy," taunted Ko. "That 'weak' creature brings all my cards back to life!"

"What just happened?" Mimi asked.

Rekuta shuddered as he explained. "Gigargon can bring back two cards from the player's graveyard. Ko's hand is full again."

"That doesn't seem fair!" exclaimed Mimi.

Sayuki rolled her eyes. "Well, no, Mimi, it's not fair. But that's kind of the whole point!"

"Ready to take your medicine, loser?" Ko asked.

Knight knew that a few of Ko's Darkness Civilization cards could force some of Shobu's cards to the graveyard. But he continued to keep his mouth shut and let Shobu learn the hard way.

"Gigagiele! Attack Stonesaur!" Ko shouted.

Shobu loved that move. "You just messed up, Ko! Stonesaur, you have more power. Blow

Gigagiele away! I'm going to win!"

Ko chuckled smugly.

"That vampire giggle doesn't sound good," commented Mimi.

"You are so right," moaned Rekuta. "Gigagiele is a slayer card, dragging Shobu's mighty Stonesaur to the graveyard."

Now the action really heated up. "I cast Tornado Flame!" Shobu shouted.

"Yes!" cried Sayuki. "Shobu just destroyed Gigargon."

But Ko wasn't worried. "Stop wasting my time, boy. Here comes a spell card. Dark Reversal!"

Shobu's smile quickly evaporated. Ko was playing with him like a cat with a rubber mouse!

"Now, class, let's recap, shall we?" said Ko. "The Dark Reversal card brings my creatures back from the graveyard. Which means what, schoolboy? That's right. I get Gigargon back. Oh . . . and he'll

crush you on my next turn!"

As Knight winced, Mimi asked, "So that was a
bad move for Shobu, right?"

Rekuta had just typed the note BONEHEAD!
next to Shobu's last move as he answered Mimi.
"Yes, Mimi, crushing someone is very bad."

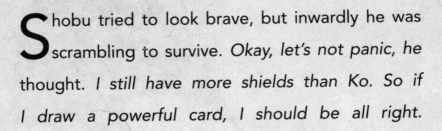

Shobu tried to look brave, but inwardly he was scrambling to survive. *Okay, let's not panic, he* thought. *I still have more shields than Ko. So if I draw a powerful card, I should be all right.*

Shobu drew a card and continued to plan his strategy. *Great! It's Bolshack Dragon! He's about to save my behind. But I should wait and see what Ko's going to do before I use this card.* Shobu called out, "I summon Onslaughter Triceps!"

Ko called Shobu's bluff. "Obviously no one has taught you the Duel Masters poker face,

schoolboy. I could tell by your expression that you just pulled a good card."

"Uh . . . um . . . no, I didn't."

"Oh, yes, you did."

"Did not."

"Did too."

"You're wrong."

"Am not. I know everything. I'm an evil genius."

"Fine. Then prove it!"

"I shall," replied Ko confidently. "I think I'll use . . . hmm, let's see. How about Ghost Touch? You'll likely recognize it as another spell card, won't you, Sho-boo-boo? Or haven't you learned that much about the game yet?"

Shobu quickly realized the consequences of Ko's latest move. He screamed.

Shobu's loud cry of agony was followed by Ko's long squeal of happiness. "Ghost Touch can send one of the cards in Shobu's hand to the grave-yard," Ko said. "Ghost Touch, take his Bolshack Dragon card!"

Shobu was going down fast. "Bolshack's gone?" he groaned. "I thought good guys were sup-posed to win!"

"Stop whimpering . . . wimp!" said Ko. "I want you to focus as I prove my evil genius status. I sum-mon Swamp Worm! Let's send Triceps to the grave-yard as well!"

Shobu shook nervously as his mind raced. *Bolshack and Triceps gone? I don't think I can win. Is it getting dark?*

Ko is taking over, thought Knight. *Come on, kid. Fight his mind games!*

"Something wrong, mousse-head?" Ko taunt-ed. "It's your turn."

Shobu tried to shake off the stupor. He shout-ed, "I summon Gatling Skyterror!"

Knight winced and shook his head. *That's the wrong move! The kid forgot he sent a mana card to his graveyard when he summoned Triceps. Now he doesn't have enough mana.*

"No, Shobu!" shouted Sayuki. "That's a mistake even beginners don't make!"

"We are done," Ko proclaimed.

"No! Let me try again!" pleaded Shobu.

Ko sneered and shook his head. "That's enough. To think I've been dueling with someone so incompetent that he doesn't even know the basic rules. You are an embarrassment and not even worth destroying. This duel never happened. Understand what I'm saying?"

Shobu was crushed and embarrassed. He slumped to the ground, fighting back tears. "I . . . really . . . messed . . . that . . . up."

Ko fired one last shot before walking away. "Look at little Sho-boo-hoo crying. Another imposter destroyed. And we didn't even finish the duel."

Shobu's friends surrounded him. "Are you all right?" Rekuta asked.

Sayuki shook her head. "This does not bode well for his future."

Knight kept his thoughts to himself: *The kid's lost in the darkness.*

9

The next day, at the card shop, Rekuta gave his father an update on Shobu. "He's one depressed duel-meister, Pop."

"When we left him at school," added Sayuki, "his head was buried in his locker — avoiding everyone's taunts. One kid shouted at him, 'Hey Kirafuda! You don't duel — you drool!'"

"Nothing's going to perk him up," said Rekuta, sighing.

"We'll see about that," said Mimi. "Here he comes — and I've got a little Duel Masters humor to boost his spirits!"

Shobu wandered into the shop, moping.

Mimi immediately approached him. "Hey, Shobu! Here's today's Duel Masters quiz question! If Gatling Skyterror had a dog, what would they name his card?"

Barely listening, Shobu mumbled, "I don't know, Mimi."

Mimi bounced in anticipation of delivering the punch line. "It would be Gatling Skyterrier! Hee hee! Get it? Dog? Sky*terrier*?"

"Nice going, Mimi," muttered Sayuki. "You just reminded him of the card he lost the match with!"

"Oops!" said Mimi, her eyes bugging wide. "My bad!"

Rekuta's father whispered, "Let me talk to him."

The kids nodded and wandered off to watch

some duels underway in the shop.

"I hear this Ko is a pretty tough cookie, Shobu," said Rekuta's father.

Shobu was honest with his oldest fan. "He's better than tough. He seems invincible. Maybe if I just had more Darkness cards, I could —"

"You're forgetting what true dueling is all about!" interrupted the shop owner. "You can't just play from your head, you have to play with your heart. You want all the glory of a Duel Master, without the work. If you don't mind my saying, you were a pretty arrogant kid who just took a whipping from Kokujoh."

"He told me he'd make me want to quit . . . and he was right," Shobu admitted.

"You tanked yesterday. So what?" asked Rekuta's father. "Today's another day. You won't make that mistake again. And you don't need a Darkness deck. You're the son of Shori Kirafuda —

one of the greatest Duel Masters ever born. I can't tell you how many world championship duels he won on his wits and faith in himself when he didn't have the deck. I remember once your dad was facing doom, with his opponent threatening to use Hanusa —"

"Whoa!" Shobu broke in. "That's the strongest double-breaker card!"

"Right!" Rekuta's father said. "And your father used Rothus, the Traveler. It's a small card, but it can send an opposing player to the graveyard. Since the mighty Hanusa was the only opponent creature left, your dad won the match. But you should know that your dad got to those championship duels on the back of many losses over the years."

"How can you be a champion if you're a loser?" asked Shobu.

"Simple. Believe in yourself. Never give up. And you'll *always* win!"

"What do you mean?"

"Let the losses make you a stronger player," replied the shop owner. "Absorb new attack and defense strategies from the duelers who occasionally squash you." Rekuta's dad smiled. "Now take what you learned yesterday and go send Ko back to Kokomo!"

Shobu brightened. "You're right! I can do this. Today I *will* own the zone!"

10

A vicious cackle echoed in the distance as Shobu and his friends arrived at the park. A demolished player staggered past them.

"Looks like Ko made another go," Sayuki said.

Ko spied Shobu approaching and dissed him immediately. "What are you doing here, schoolboy? I believe I expelled you yesterday."

"You afraid to play me again?" Shobu challenged.

"Why would I fear a dueler dud like you?" Ko replied.

"'Cause I'm a dueler *dude*, with a deck to prove it!"

"Got some new cards?" Ko asked.

"Nope. A new attitude."

"But you lack my *altitude*, schoolboy," said Ko, with his evil chuckle. Then he sighed and nodded. "Okay, loser, bring on your best."

As the match progressed, Rekuta saw that the duelers' decks seemed equally strong. Shobu held back, putting cards in his mana zone. This made Ko impatient. "Kid, this is a duel, not a tea party. What are you waiting for?"

Shobu kept his cool and just smiled.

Ko was impressed. "Okay, kid, you're smarter than you were yesterday. But don't get too cocky. I've kicked your butt once and I'll be one step ahead of you."

"Maybe you won't," Shobu answered confidently.

"Well, if you won't attack me, I might as well get this party started," said Ko. "I attack with Gigagiele! Plus Bone Spider . . . and Bone Assassin! Break his shields — now!"

Mimi squealed. "Oh no! Shobu's shields are history!"

Ko's grim giggle returned. "Speaking of history, it looks like yesterday's disaster is repeating itself . . . Schmo-bu!"

"But I'm a schmo with mo', creepy one," Shobu shot back, "and I summon Meteosaur! And Gatling Skyterror!"

"Is that the best you can do?" asked Ko, with a smirk.

"Nope," Shobu replied. "Start quaking, because I attack Bone Spider with Immortal Baron Vorg!"

Rekuta liked the moves he was typing into his laptop. "You're the man, Shobu!"

Ko's lip twitched a bit. "Not bad, rookie," he said with a grudging sneer.

"Did I detect a compliment, monster man?" inquired Shobu. "Well, save it, because there's more! Meteorsaur . . . attack Bone Assassin!"

Ko yawned. "Ho hum. Bloody Squito! Block the very lame Meteorsaur!"

"Hang in there, Shobu," cried Mimi, "you can beat him!"

Sayuki preferred another brand of motivation. "You lose to the same guy twice, Sho baby, and I may have to reconsider my social circles!"

"You won't have to switch friends, Sayuki," said Shobu with a smile, "because tough guy here seems to have run out of shields. Watch as the fun begins!" He faced Ko. "You put up a heck of a fight, partner. Now why don't you just go home and practice your evil laugh for the rest of the day? You're goin' down . . . now!" Then he put down a card.

"Fatal Attacker Horvath — go get Bone Assassin!

As Rekuta typed what he thought was a game-winning move into the computer, everyone cheered.

Everyone but Kokujo, that is. His evil snicker quickly wiped the smiles off their faces.

Chapter 11

With a smirk, Ko declared, "I've got you right where I want you. I summon Deathliger, Lion of Chaos!"

Rekuta's fingers froze on the keyboard. "Not Deathliger!" he gasped. "That's a double-breaker!"

"Your friend's right," said Ko, with his finest monster laugh. "It's time to wipe that cocky little smile off your face, Kirifuda. Too bad you had to learn the hard way that the bigger the creatures in your deck, the bigger your Duel Masters victory!"

Shobu wasn't ready to quit the fevered battle.

"My father's a world class Duel Master and he says, 'No matter what you have in your deck, believe in yourself and you'll always win!'"

"So, do you believe in yourself today, Grasshopper?" Ko asked.

"Yep," answered Shobu, "*and* Magma Gazer . . . who I command to give power to Gatling Skyterror!"

Ko did a double take at the board. "What the . . . ?"

"Shobu's still in the game!" cried Sayuki. "Magma Gazer can power up a creature in the battle zone!"

Typing frantically, Rekuta added, "Gatling Skyterror's power is increased by 4000!"

"Is that good?" asked Mimi.

"It's awesome!" cried Rekuta. "Now Shobu can win!"

Shobu prepared to put Ko away. "Now who's asleep? Gatling Skyterror — destroy!"

Shobu's friends went ballistic, cheering wildly.

Kokujo was befuddled. "What just happened here?"

"Do the math, duel loser!" said Shobu. "A smaller creature can beat a larger one if you really know what you're doing. A very wise man taught me that. And now, you'll pardon me while I blow you away! I summon Bolshack Dragon to break shields!"

But Ko wasn't ready to lose this seesaw battle. "Did you think I would just roll over and surrender that easily? I summon Bone Spider! And Death Smoke, go get Bolshack Dragon! Now, Swamp Worm, destroy his shields!"

What an incredible battle this had become! Once again, the tables turned quickly, leaving Shobu's cheerleaders silenced in shock — with sore necks, too, from turning back and forth like this was a tennis match!

"Shobu's only got one shield left," moaned Mimi.

Meanwhile, Rekuta typed a note into his game record. It read: SHOBU DOOMED NOW.

Shobu didn't panic. He'd planned his next move. "I love the sound of armor being crushed! Gatling Skyterror, break his shields!"

"He did it!" shouted Sayuki.

"Ready to give up now, Kokujo?" Shobu asked confidently.

"Are you?" answered Ko, unruffled. "Because I have you right where I want now."

Shobu shook his head, confused. Kokujo was beaten . . . wasn't he?

No, he wasn't.

"Terror Pit was hiding in my shield," Ko declared. "Go, Terror Pit! Now we're getting down to business! Creatures, final attack!"

Shobu groaned.

It was over.

He'd lost to Kokujo.

Again.

12

Shobu slumped down and buried his head between his knees. His whole body shook from what appeared to be uncontrollable sobbing.

Ko didn't mind taunting the loser as he laughed. "And you thought you'd won! I was toying with you all along! Oh . . . and your dueling banter needs a lot of work, Schmo-bu. 'I believe in myself,' you said. Didn't do you much good, did it?"

Kokujo turned and strutted away. As he left the park, he muttered to himself, "Man, that kid's got potential! He'll never know how close he came to actually beating me."

Meanwhile, Shobu's friends rushed to his side, concerned that his Duel Masters days were over. "Are you all right?" asked Rekuta.

"Shobu! Say something!" pleaded Mimi.

"Come on, pal," said Sayuki, patting Shobu's back. "Stop crying. It's okay."

Shobu popped his head up with a big smile. He wasn't crying. He was shaking with laughter! "Guys, I'm fine!" he said. "Sure, I'm bummed that I lost. But that's the deal! Sometimes you win, sometimes you lose! But when you try your hardest . . . man, what a rush!"

"So, you're okay?" asked Mimi.

"I'm more than okay!" shouted Shobu. "That black-coated freak gave me the duel of a lifetime, and I want to feel this way again and again. I want to be the best — just like my dad!"

It was obvious Shobu had finally seen the

light. As the friends left the park, he happily declared, "Yep! Never again will this Duel Master park in the dark!"

Fuel the Duel

Get the Duel Masters™ 2 Player Starter Set, packed with everything you need to start playing right away!

DUEL MASTERS
TRADING CARD GAME ™